CRYBABY

by Jacquie Hann

You might find someone who is a little bit like you in this picture book. Maybe you have tried to find out what's wrong so that you can help a friend stop crying! Or maybe you've acted like Older Brother, laughing and teasing. And maybe sometimes, when you don't really know why, something happens to make you cry.

CRYBABY

CRYBABY

by Jacquie Hann

FOUR WINDS PRESS

NEW YORK

Library of Congress Cataloging in Publication Data

Hann, Jacquie.
  Crybaby.

  SUMMARY: A child starts to cry after a disagreement
with his mother and has difficulty stopping.
  [1. Crying — Fiction] I. Title.
PZ7.H19646Cr   [E]   78-22035
ISBN 0-590-07609-4

Published by Four Winds Press
A division of Scholastic Magazines, Inc., New York, N.Y.
Copyright © 1979 by Jacquie Hann
All rights reserved
Printed in the United States of America
Library of Congress Catalog Card Number: 78-22035
1   2   3   4   5   83   82   81   80   79

For Aunt Milly and Uncle Carl,
who always understood kids

CRYBABY

Sometimes when my mother and I don't agree

I close my eyes
and bite my lip
and sniff my nose

but the tears just flow.

"Stop that silly crying," my mother says.

I hold my breath.
I wipe my eyes.
"I'm trying," I say.

More tears roll down my face.

My mother says crying makes me red as a lobster.

My father says I look wet as a fish.

My brother says I look like a baboon, even without crying.

I start howling like a lone wolf.

Then my mother tries to make me smile.

My father tries to make me laugh.

My brother just makes things worse
so I cry even harder.

Then my mother asks me what's so terrible.

My father says he'll kiss it better.

My brother tries to make me madder.

I think I'll cry forever.

My mother says I can have a triple decker ice cream fling.

My father says he'll tell me the preposterous panda story.

My brother says he'll eat my triple decker ice cream fling.

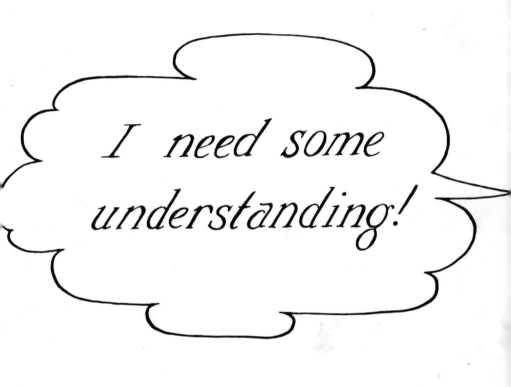

My mother says my crying makes her sad.

My father says it makes him feel bad.

That makes me feel a little better.

I blow my nose.
I wipe my eyes.

And even though my brother tries

he doesn't make me cry.